T 64206

S0-BUC-556

DISCARD

Sweeney Elementary School Library
Shakopee, Minnesota

The Seal and the Slick

Sweeney Elementary School Library

Shakopee Minnesota

The Seal

and the Slick

Sweeney Elementary School Library
Shakopee, Minnesota

Story and pictures by

Don Freeman

The Viking Press   New York

To
Larry Pidgeon
Ken Millar
Lois Sidenberg
and
Bud Bottoms

First Edition
Copyright © 1974 by Don Freeman. All rights reserved.
First published in 1974 by The Viking Press, Inc., 625 Madison Avenue, New York, N.Y. 10022.
Published simultaneously in Canada by The Macmillan Company of Canada Limited.
Library of Congress catalog card number: 73–16118   Pic Bk   SBN 670-62659-7
1 2   3   4   5   78   77   76   75   74

It is a gray misty morning on Seal Rock Island.

A family of carefree sea lions awaken. They are in no hurry to begin the day. There is plenty of time for swimming, fishing, and playing.

Soon the rays of the sun melt away the mist.
The seals watch the cormorants and the pelicans dive into the
blue-green waters for their breakfasts.

Far across the channel gleams the beautiful
harbor town of Pacifica.
But is it as serene as it appears?

The father sea lion suddenly lifts his nose into the air and sniffs.
His white whiskers twitch. The mother sea lion knows this means
he smells danger! Out comes a loud bellowing bark, a warning.

The youngest and friskiest pup perks up his small ears. He too points his nose into the air and sniffs. He catches a whiff of something different. Where is it coming from — the land? Or from the sea?

He dives off the rock into the clear bright water
to go exploring on his own.

The other seals know better. They don't dare go against their father's warning.

Deeper and deeper the pup descends.

Fish stream past. They seem frightened, not of him but of something else. There is a strange thumping, pumping sound.

Suddenly the pup finds himself surrounded by darkness. He swims upward, where everything is black. No sunlight shines through from above.

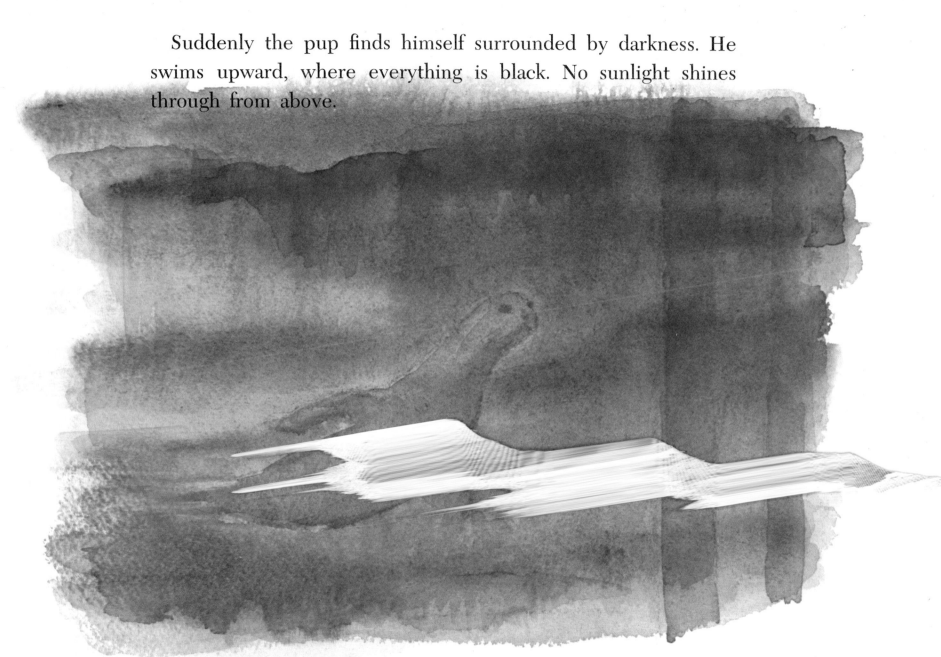

To catch his breath, the seal surfaces. His flippers are heavy with a sticky goo.

Is that a giant sea monster standing on long legs?

No. It is an oil well spouting a cloud of dark steam.

There has been a blowout! Yellow-black oil is seeping up from the ocean floor.

The poor young seal is caught in the slick!

Bravely he struggles to stay afloat. The incoming tide gradually helps carry him ashore.

He rests on the wet sand, barely able to move. Alone and far from home, he tries to bark.

A girl and boy come running across the sand dunes.
They are looking for sea birds that might be in trouble.

They examine the pup's fur. "He's covered with thick, icky oil," says the girl. "He won't live if we don't do something quick!"
"Let's get some fresh water!" says the boy.

First they roll the seal onto the boy's rubber raft and pull it up onto the dry sand, away from the rising tide. Then they race off to the Rescue Station at the harbor.

Workmen are spreading bushels of straw along the shoreline to soak up the oil from the blackened beach.

Fishermen are scooping up globs of oil from the water.

Young people are doing their best to clean the sea birds found lying on the sand, helpless and dying.

"Come on! Hurry!" shouts the boy. "We have to save our seal!"

Sweeney Elementary School Library
Shakopee, Minnesota

They bring back buckets of fresh water, two scrub brushes, and
a bottle of special cleaning fluid and begin scrubbing the seal's
flippers. Then they try to wipe the oil from his head and body.

Soon they need more fresh water.
Once again they race back to the Rescue Station.

Meanwhile the waves are coming nearer and nearer.
Now the rubber raft has spun around and is heading out to sea.

The seal pup is riding along like a real surfer!

But not for long.
He slides off the raft and begins to swim toward his island home.

Being a much wiser pup than he was this morning, he keeps a
safe distance away from the terrible slick.

The boy and girl return and find their sea lion gone.
"He swam away!" they both shout. "He's saved! We saved him!"
"And here comes my raft back!" cries the boy in surprise.
Then, without saying another word, they race back to help
save the birds.

Finally the young explorer arrives home.
But there is no one in sight!

He climbs from rock to rock, searching everywhere.

All at once he stops. His flippers step on something firm and mossy, not at all like a jagged rock. . . .

It's his father!

The grand old sea lion raises himself up and gives a loud, happy-sounding *yap!* Then he flaps his flippers, and suddenly

the mother seal and all the other seals appear.

Now the father gives a signal. And together the family swims to another island home, far away from the dangerous slick.

The youngest pup is the last to climb ashore. He is very tired. Small wonder he is the first one to stretch out on the sand and fall fast asleep.